Ray Nelms: A Study in Insanity

Rebel Wayfarers MC & Freed Riders MC Crossover

MariaLisa deMora

Edited by Hot Tree Editing

First Published 2018

ISBN 13: 978-1-946738-14-1

DEDICATION

In this version of reality folks don't get to
pick out their family, so this
story is dedicated to mine.
You got lucky!

CONTENTS

ACKNOWLEDGMENTS

For a long time I've wondered about the bad guys in my dreams. Exactly how did they turn out the way they are, and the heros take a different path? Is it nature, bred deep in their bones? Or could it be strictly nurture, stained into their souls from the time they stood at the knees of those who raised them? Could their journey have been altered, given the right push at the right time?

Age old questions, right?

Still. I wonder.

Ray Nelms is one of those bad guys who just won't be quiet. Even way back when I was telling Duck's story, Ray seemed to long for his fifteen minutes of fame, breaking through and into Duck's dreams. And because I wonder … now here he is, given center stage in his own story.

Is the attention deserved? Well, I guess you'll have to be the judge of that, won't you?

If you get a minute, let me know, would ya?

Woofully yours,

~ML

Ray Nelms: A Study in Insanity

What thoughts go through the mind of a psychopath when they know they're about to die? Is it a gloating recitation of favored successes, or an internal rendition of failures? For Ray Nelms, the peace knowing his pain is about to end grants him insight into how he became the monster he hated.

***

Ray Nelms wasn't born a monster. He had a fairly banal young childhood in West Texas, trailing around after the older brother he idolized. Ray didn't enter the world evil. No. He was made that way.

A character warped at the hands of his father, a young Ray was guided on the first tentative steps down the path of darkness in an effort to save his brother. Reuben was everything good in the world, and Ray desperately wanted him to stay that way.

Through the years, the wicked machinations of his paternal mentor branded twisted trails into Ray's psyche, leaving him always searching for the next intoxicating high.

Only Ray's addiction wasn't borne on illicit drugs. It came from a place deep inside him, where the blackness clamored for violence and blood.

Through the years, he kept it fed very well.

This is the tale of how it finally came to an end.

Abbreviation map:

- RWMC – Rebel Wayfarers MC
- FRMC – Freed Riders MC

The End of Matters

Staring at the dim shadows traveling a predictable route and pace across the vehicle's ceiling, Ray Nelms felt a sense of tranquility and an unfamiliar peace. For a change, his brain wasn't running circles around in his head, chasing its own tail.

Instead of a thousand plans, there was only one thing on his mind.

Everything has a cycle. Even me. Time to close the gate on the arena. We're all done here. Moving on.

As the van's suspension bounced and swayed, the bindings made it so he could simply go with the motion, and he rolled gently side to side like tiny wavelets crawling up the seashore. It was not dissimilar to the natural way his body would move when he was in complete sync with a bull he'd ride the full way into the eight-second ending.

Bull riding had always been a means to an end for him. Even from the beginning, it had been about besting the animal, of course. But it was also a chance to conveniently place himself into the path of others who also chose the isolating career. When a person was on the road eight or nine months out of the year, chasing buckles and checks, it was easy for one of them to simply drop out of sight.

That was why he'd been down in Houston. He'd set his sights on a goal. A prize.

The only prize that ever mattered.

Then it was snatched out of his grip by rough men who rode motorcycles instead of bulls.

Assholes. Still. Jesus, I'm glad Reuben wasn't there. No, not Reuben, he's Duck now, I need to remember the name. Real glad he didn't get to see me like this.

The disappointment on his big brother's face would have killed him. Even now, seeing it only through his imagination, Ray's stomach soured.

He's the only one who ever thought I was worth anything. All that's stopping now, though. Tonight's gonna be it for me.

He pulled in as deep a breath as he could, trussed up like a roped calf. Old injuries ached with the movement, the pain a constant backdrop to the agony that would fill his brain at times. Another breath brought with it the stench of his own sweat. He ignored the smell and aches, trying to allow his brain to stay dormant.

This was freedom—knowing the pain he'd carried for so long was about to end.

Now that he was no longer in the grip of the frenzied need that had come over him on the Harris County fairgrounds, Ray could see clearly where everything had gone wrong. Not just for tonight in Houston, but perhaps throughout his life.

Been a long time coming. I've been messed up for so long, I can't remember any other way.

He suspected if he'd ever bothered to see a shrink, they could have done a bang-up job pinpointing where things had gone off the rails.

Woulda had a field day shrinking me. "Now tell me about your father?" Jesus. If I'd told them everything, they'd have shit their pants right then and there. Facing down a monster, they'd have had their moment of clarity in flight-or-fight mode. Now me? I'm a fighter from way back.

It wouldn't have taken a genius to see where nature had met nurture in such a damaging and abrupt way that it had thrown the entire rest of his life askew.

Ray had done enough casual research into his own quirks and problems that he knew all the words. He was able to readily spout off about various diagnoses and labels that would likely have been applied to him as a kid. No way around it, really. After doing the things he'd done—*been made to do*—and seeing what he'd seen? Hell yeah, a shrink would have been sympathetic. And dismayed. No doubt. They'd have wept for the man he could have been even as they signed the orders locking him away forever.

This way is cleaner. Lots less time to contemplate the kind of man I've become. Reuben got the good genes. Thank God for that, at least. Here I sit, the twisted spawn of the devil himself. But Rue? He's a damn good man.

"Nothing that happened to me was his fault." The words were wheezed out from his tortured throat, voice pitched two octaves higher than normal. Ray bit down on his tongue before his traitorous mouth could respond further to the ghost voices in his head, tasting bright copper as his teeth tore the flesh.

Phantoms in my head. Like I'm haunted. I wonder if this is how Daddy felt.

Daddy.

His fingers twitched involuntarily as if they were once again wrapped around that age-wizened neck. The old man hadn't fought it.

Knew it was his time, I guess.

With his last breath, his father had lifted one ice-cold hand, curling fragile fingers around Ray's wrist, the pressure of that grip so weak it was laughable.

The only way to curb that man was to kill him. Patricide hasn't been the curse I expected it to be. No regrets from me. Old man had to die. Hell, he shoulda died a long time earlier. Things might have been different if I'd just nutted up and taken care of business.

Once he'd gotten things ramped up with Ray, the old man had taken to going to Mexico, down past the bridge and into the warren of streets that could lead to paradise or hell, depending on your poison. Expanding his hunting fields into that foreign land.

That was during one of those times I tried so hard to stuff it in a box. Tried so hard. Failed hard too.

The sickness that lived inside him would eat at him for weeks and months at a time. This was back before he knew that denying the need only made it grow stronger. It had gotten to the point that just the smell following his father home after a trip down to Mexico had been enough to wake the beast within Ray.

Sex, depravity, blood, and terror.

Had to kill him.

A man seated nearby turned to stare out the van's back doors. He announced, "We're clear," as if everyone would understand what that meant.

Someone in the front of the van responded, "Two more fences. Wanna get well away from the roads."

Smart.

They weren't from Reuben's—*Duck's*—group. But Ray was glad he was being bested by someone who at least seemed to know their shit when it came to disposing bodies.

I could still probably teach 'em a thing or two. Bet I've got their count beaten by a bunch of numbers. Double digits, at least.

He snorted at the mental competition, taking care to keep it quiet. But the idea stayed, waking up a tiny part of his brain.

Wonder how many total I've killed? Can I even put a number on it after all this time?

Closing his eyes to focus, he quickly lost himself amid remembered details of favorite scenes. Well-worn paths of imagery that were burned into his brain, not only from each event but also from studying photographs he'd taken. Treasured trophies he'd kept safe, only bringing those precious images out when the need rode heavy on him. He'd flip through the pictures, hoping the evidence of his exquisite handiwork would keep those dark and twisted desires at arm's length. Trying to hold off as long as he could.

So much to remember.

He'd always remember.

To my dying day.

One Memory

The brunette had struggled, her wiry strength a surprise, making besting her an exciting challenge. She'd come willingly to Ray's trailer, and then given her body over to him in a show of trust. As a gift, he'd gotten her off, working her with skill until she cried out, overwhelmed by the sensations.

Now that he had his hands on her, Ray could see she was just a stand-in for Mica Scott. Her rounded face was turning red in the heated air of the trailer, brightly flushed skin framed by black locks. Shadows from the uncertain lighting made her cheekbones look even more prominent, the First Nation blood rearing its head.

He didn't intend to kill her.

Not yet.

He'd been planning this game for weeks, following her around the circuit, and learning everything he could about her. After putting in the time, there was no way he wanted to cut his fun short. Sure, all that work meant he'd learned what she liked, but even more critical to his plan, he'd taken care to learn her fears.

Everyone had a fear that could cripple. *Everything,* he mentally corrected himself.

It's not about her being a woman. I kill men just as easy. She's just a means to an end.

Ray casually adjusted his hold on her, the blood that kept her alive coursing rapidly just millimeters underneath his hand.

"You're afraid," he murmured, watching as bright red bloomed in one eye, staining the sclera in an uneven oval. "Afraid of losing. What a joke."

That had been the goad to get her to this event, him telling her all about how the biggest names would pass the show by, leaving easy points for the picking.

"Wasn't wrong. I didn't lie to you about that."

Her movements slowed, then stopped, and he relaxed his grip slightly, rewarded when her body reflexively pulled in a breath so deep, her back arched.

Thumb to her carotid, he waited, feeling her pulse even out slowly but surely. Then her eyes fluttered open, and the instant after her gaze landed on him, that oh-so gentle thrum raced again.

"Afraid of losing, and now—" He tightened his grip, pushing his thumb deeper into her flesh, satisfied with the feel of it giving under the power of his hand. "—you're afraid of me."

For his game, the location selected had been critical, because these particular fairgrounds butted up against a pork operation. There were two stories of confinement hogs waiting out their lives with restricted movement, carefully monitored diets, and artificially constructed days. Waiting for their meals, they'd happily accept an out-of-cycle one.

Everything was going to work out as he'd planned.

Stuff all the bad inside this box I'm making and hide it away.

***

Circling back through the town a few weeks later, he'd picked up a copy of the local newspaper to see if the missing woman had been found.

Just a few parts of her.

Seemed pigs didn't digest teeth. Wasn't like it was enough to identify her. Hell, from what he could tell, no one even knew the woman was missing yet. The teeth were just an unidentified person who'd met a terrible end falling in a hog pen.

But he'd known.

Still, I learned something for the future. Good thing I've always been a student of the trade. I'm forever willin' to add to my bank of knowledge.

***

Knowledge had been an important component of all his games. Know your target, know your surroundings, know your plan A and plan B, and know your escape route.

Right now, in the back of a van hogtied with ankles bound to wrists, Ray was trussed up like a zealot missionary on a cannibal's spit.

Pretty sure I can't plan my way out of this one.

When he'd taken Mica for the last time, he'd violated every one of his rules. Even as he'd done it, the flaws in his lack of planning had mocked him. Where he was right now was his own failure coming home to roost.

Hogtied.

He snorted again.

Always comes back to the hogs, I guess. At least long pig's not my kink.

That thought stirred another memory, curdled in a far corner of his brain.

For a time, he had associated with a man who got off on biting the women they'd shared. Latching tight, the bastard would clamp down hard, coming up for air with blood on his teeth and gums, lips painted red. That was during a period when Ray had most missed the work done alongside his father. An image of Reuben flashed through his head—*their* father. It had been hard to run all alone, and he had hoped the biting man would fill that singing need for a true partner.

The man didn't. He couldn't.

In the end, he'd been just another disposal site marked on a map kept reverently in a drawer in the trailer.

The trailer of doom. Wonder what they'll make of my stuff?

Ray had learned to carefully store the most sensitive tools in the climate-controlled apartment section of his horse trailer. Those expensive and specialized toys that needed particular care to remain effective.

He'd taken care to conduct his research using anonymous computer kiosks, then purchased the necessary items in well-trafficked, out of the way places, his face made forgettable unless he wanted to be remembered.

I played the part of a white hat through and through when I was on supply runs like that.

Even the more common tools—these not being ones for rodeo or construction, but for slaughterhouses—were tucked into a container wedged deep in the locked toolbox of his truck.

They'll look there, I'm sure. These men aren't stupid, and I know I would if I were them. They're gonna find everything. I kinda hope they do.

The few chemicals he'd used were stored in plain sight, placed near the feed bin alongside tubs of vitamins for the horses he occasionally hauled for pay. As a bull rider, he didn't need to drag a trailer to transport his own livestock, but he'd liked the freedom having a mobile base of operations gave him.

He imagined the looks on the faces of the Rebel Wayfarers as they dug through his stash. Mica'd found a group of competent guardians in that RWMC crew. He'd noticed that the man sitting over him didn't wear their patch, and this example of the extent of the Rebel's reach hadn't escaped Ray's scrutiny.

Sure. Now I figure it out. Day late and a dollar short. Those fuckers have been everywhere I showed up for the past several months. I hate knowing I underestimated them.

The how of why Mica had hitched her wagon to the motorcycle club was lost in the distant past. Then, when Ray had found out Reuben had joined the exact same club, it had felt like fate had tied all their destinies tightly together.

Fates. Those bitches have been steadily tugging on fraying threads to pull me in. Fucking bitches.

The trailer would be gone over with a fine-toothed comb, no doubt. Once they got into the depths of it, he hoped someone realized how dedicated and diligent he'd been.

If he were still around, their questions would be urgent, if predictable. "So, Ray, exactly how many have there been? How many have you killed?"

More than you've got teeth in your head, cowboy.

He closed his eyes, going back to digging through the only trophies now at his beck and call: memories.

At three-dozen remembered murders, Ray gave up counting, abandoning his obscene cataloging.

Instead, he turned his mind to the beginning, and those first frustrating failures.

The ones like fucking Mica. Like her sister, Molly Scott. Like Anabelle Taylor, Lisa Kennwort, and Tiffany Wabash.

The ones who got away.

The familiar curl of fear crawled up his spine, wrapping around so it settled in his belly.

Failure should have been disallowed.

Failure meant there was someone in the world who knew dark secrets about him, something he'd been schooled from twelve to never allow.

He remembered.

How It Started

On nights when their father had a visitor in his shed, the hallway stretching the length of the house always felt twice as long.

Twelve-year-old Ray dragged each step he took, holding to every slow second before he had to face the window in his room. Wooden-framed thin glass, the single panes did nothing to hold back the grotesque sounds that would be emanating from the shed in the backyard, that twelve-foot-square section of hell.

Tonight, it held a sweet waitress from town. A woman who'd arrived with a smile plastered on her face as she'd climbed out of the ranch truck, her fancy dress telling a tale of desire.

Ray attended school with her daughter. He wouldn't be able to look the girl in the face tomorrow.

Reuben's door opened as Ray attempted to sneak past. "He got someone?" Only a year separated them, and the boys protected each other as best they could. Ray nodded. Reuben studied him for a minute, then asked, "It gonna get bad?" Ray swallowed and nodded again. His older brother whirled and slugged the wall, puffs of plaster evidence of a hit hard enough to crack the drywall. "Why does he have to be like this?" Turning back, Reuben stared at him for a minute. "Someone's got to stop him. One of these times he's going to really hurt someone. Hurt 'em bad."

Ray saw the courage his brother pulled together and knew he couldn't allow what Reuben was about to do. With the way their father felt about Reuben, his dark soul full of an unreasonable hatred of his firstborn son, Ray's brother going out and interrupting things would mean more than a beating for him. It could mean...anything.

Once their father was in the grip of his compulsion, being in his way was one of the most dangerous places to be.

Their ranch foreman had done that last year, pounding on the shed's door, shouting for Nelms to stop.

His father's game had been with the foreman's daughter that time, making the man's urgency entirely understandable as he tried to halt the train wreck from happening. Instead, it had turned into wreckage of a different kind.

Through the same thin glass, Ray had watched as their father loaded a tarp-covered bundle into the back of the truck. When he'd driven away, Ray had covertly followed him down the cart track to the gully where they dumped dead cows refused by the renderer. He'd then watched as the foreman's limp body tumbled to the bottom. A cascade of rotting carcasses had followed him down, covering the corpse in moments.

All for nothing.

One night later, the girl had been back in the shed, her screams finding no hero that time.

"I'll go," Ray said suddenly, not knowing where the words came from. "He doesn't hate me as much."

"No," Reuben argued. "You don't need to see that."

Ray laughed.

Six hours later, he'd stumbled back upstairs. His hair, clothes...hell, his skin smelled of smokes, booze, and sex. Reuben had been waiting and the moment he'd laid eyes Ray, it was as if a door closed in his face.

From that night on, Reuben had hated him.

19

Continued Corruption

Was that really the beginning of the end? Way back then?

The van rolled across another cattle guard, bringing him still closer to what would become his last resting place. The man above him stared out the back window, jaw clenched.

The very act of dominating had been heady at first. Ray liked the rush of commanding another being and having them readily do his bidding.

His father had treated him as a collaborator, someone to eagerly bounce ideas around with. One night, when he was well into his whiskey, Ray's father shared how just overhearing what they would be doing seemed to ratchet up the tension for their partners. Ray understood the importance of the pageant then, the build-up of nerves made the end release so much better. For the women, but also for him.

The death of the foreman seemed an aberrant slip in his father's process, and Ray had trusted that his father knew best. He pushed the memory far to the back of his mind, finding a box to shove it into for storage.

Locked away.

It was only much later that Ray had realized those first months were tame compared to what their father had been used to doing.

He'd been easing me into the role I cast for myself.

When he thought about the pain and suffering they'd caused, for a long time Ray had mentally excused their actions because, as his father had said time and again, the women came to them. These were consensual, agreed-upon encounters. The women had been seeking a source of safe kink. It was far different from what their husbands might find down in Mexico.

We weren't so bad, in comparison.

In his head, Ray had believed all of that meant his role in the games was normal behavior. Even as things kept edging closer and closer to the black boundaries, it was normal. After all, the women got the darkness they asked for. Twelve-year-old Ray had held to that.

They'd asked for it.

The first time the old man killed one of their partners, it had come as a shock.

Ray had watched as his father's large, calloused hands wrapped around the woman's neck until her face purpled, the color matching her bound breasts. She had thrashed as much as taut bindings allowed, and still, his father hadn't released his hold. Ray waited until she'd gone limp, and thinking she'd passed out, had joined his father in jacking off onto her immobile body. They'd striped her skin with stream after stream of white jizz. It had only been afterward that he'd realized what had happened.

I didn't sleep for a week. He pressed his lips together. *Such a newbie racked with guilt. Such a waif.*

Weeks had gone by, where his father acted as if everything was still normal. Ray had ridden in the truck's cab out to the dead-animal gully and had been the one to roll her body down the slope.

Normal my ass.

Somewhere in there, Ray had stopped trying to sleep, because every time he closed his eyes, he was met with the sight of the woman's body. In his dreams, he'd felt again the sick relief of his release splattering against her skin.

Every hard-on had been pummeled into submission. A hard fist to the groin helped stall the pulses of desire. Finally, delirious with fatigue and shame, Ray had burned the shed in a fit of remorse. Only then had he been able to sleep.

And he'd slept like the dead.

Their father had blamed Reuben, beaten him within an inch of his life. Ray hadn't spoken up to save him, causing himself another burden of sorrow and humiliation. Rue had known, of course, and that had been just another stone laid on his own path away from Ray and the ranch.

And in the end, burning the damned shed didn't change a single thing about what happened, except the future location of the playtimes.

Older now, and with a deeper understanding the amount of work and planning that went into building something like their father'd had in the shed, Ray knew his father's reaction was mild.

It was me, I woulda killed whoever did it, even Rue.

That first murder had been the turning point for everything, an act that bound him so tightly to their father, Ray knew in his bloody gut he'd never get free.

Rue could, though. Made sure of that. Just not me. Wasn't my fate.

Each night with his father had been spent building on previous experiences, all joining together to open that gaping dark inside him wider.

Been filled with poison so long, don't know what it'd feel like to be clean.

Lessa. Sweet Lessa. She was the closest I ever came.

His wife had been clean, through and through.

Loved her, much as I was able.

When Ray married Lessa, the easy availability of even vanilla sex had relieved a portion of the dark strain inside him. As tame as the sex had been in the beginning, Lessa's sweet nature had served to ease his sickness even more.

He'd picked her out of a bar full of pretty women not for her beauty, but because she looked so much like…*Mica*. The bitch who was the reason behind him being on the floor of this van right now.

Goddamned Mica. Everything always comes back to her.

Lessa had thought she could fix him. Believed if she were sweet, pleased him in bed, cleaned his house, or was enough of anything, he'd change.

Wrong.

The bruised flesh of his lips split when they drew back across his teeth in a savage smile.

After a time, every attempt she made only served to enrage him because the actions would rile up his father. Get the old man talking about what he'd like to do to sweet Lessa. All the ways he could take her apart so much better than Ray could.

Couldn't stand to think of his hands on her. Old man hated that she was mine.

Mine.

Ray had run those months through his head repeatedly over the years, looking for but never finding a different outcome.

Once Daddy got involved, I think the end was just inevitable.

He remembered.

Loss and Insight

The coroner stalked towards him up the basement hallway in the hospital, face twisted with rage. Ray didn't know what leverage his father had over the man, but he must have something since more than one death had gotten covered up over the years. Every time, the man swore it was the last. But then Ray's father would make a call, and the man would pick up. Now, however, the coroner looked outraged.

Once he was close enough, the man reached up and slapped Ray in the chest with papers clutched in his hand, held them there and pushed hard. He forced Ray back one step, then a second before the wall caught him, holding him firm. A moment passed, then the man ground out words that echoed in Ray's head, tossing his stomach up into his throat for a moment. "She was *pregnant*."

That couldn't be right. Sure, he and Lessa talked about kids sometimes, but always in a far future sort of way. A one-day way, when life would be normal and he'd feel right about bringing another being into the world. A time when he'd be all better inside his head. After he got well. Once the sickness inside him crawled into a box and stayed there for longer than a minute.

Once Lessa finally managed to fix him.

"What?" His throat closed over the question so it came out in a broken croak, sounding like a trafficker he'd once found deep in the desert.

The dirty man had been leading underage and underdressed charges towards what would become their fresh hell. Ray'd buried his knife to the hilt under the man's chin, tongue pinned by the blade to the roof of his mouth, split soft palate working to garble his shouts and screams. Forced surgery to inflict a deadly cleft. Those kids had scattered to the winds at the sound. Ray hadn't bothered even burying that one. Scavengers hadn't had to earn their meal that night. He'd left the kids for the desert to deal with, though. That'd weighed on him for a bit.

"What do you mean?"

"Means you get pinned for this, boy, it's a double homicide."

"She can't be." Hot and heavy tears threatened, and his hitching breath clogged roughly in Ray's chest. "Not Lessa."

"She went easy," the man said, uncaring of the confusion Ray struggled through. "At least you gave her that."

"Better than letting my old man at her." Ray muttered his justification, the bitter knowledge she'd been carrying his child loosening his mouth. "Better dead than that. You sure she was pregnant?"

"Yeah, about four months along."

Four months.

That would have put conception at about the time of Ray's father's last trip to Mexico. When Ray and Lessa had the house to themselves for a week, and she'd loved up on him in that complete way that always eased the strain.

He had imagined the monster like a pustule inside him, growing larger and larger, the infection building every day until something happened to lance it off. *Rue's not this way*, he thought. *Just me. Just. Me.* "Hey, you know someone who does vasectomies?"

The man's head jerked back and he stepped away, taking the rustling papers with him. "Yeah. Why?"

"Need to kill the bloodline with me. Rue's okay, but me? I'm just like the old man. Put an end to it now."

Ultimate Rest

The van jolted, and Ray twisted his neck, rolling with the movement until he stared up at the man seated closest.

Ray watched him peer out the front windows, then turn to glare out the back before declaring, "Good a place as any." The man bent close, and Ray felt the tension ease in his arms as the rope around his ankles was removed.

And thus is decided my place of death.

"How you wanna do this?" The driver's question was barely audible over the rushing sounds of blood in Ray's ears. "We need to send them something afterwards."

Suddenly panicked at the thought of dying before he told his story, Ray stared at the man in the back of the van with him, willing him to turn around.

He didn't.

"Hey. *Hey*. You know how hard it is to get something out of your head?"

Ray's shout was cut short as his elbow caught on something when they grabbed his boots and began to drag him out. Arms stretched up over his head, the fabric of his rodeo competition shirt captured his attention for a moment. Sponsor patches competed for space, each of them had been hard won, sewn in place knowing the blood and sweat that went into a successful eight-second ride.

He kept talking, hoping someone would listen.

"Like when you go off a bull the wrong way, you can get hung up. Always seems like it takes a thousand years to loosen your knot, every jump yankin' your shoulder out of joint, fingers crushed in your glove, bull hatin' you because he can't get away from you. Over and over, and you can't get away. That's how it is. It gets locked into place and nothing can dislodge it. Hung up, hard. A lifetime."

His head impacted the van's bumper on the way down, breath knocked from his body when he landed hard on the ground. Each gasp sucked in a layer of abrasive sand, causing a cascade of coughs.

Ray croaked like a choked frog when he told them, "Mica was the key. When I had her, nothing could hold me back. Nothing could keep me down."

"Shut him up," the driver's voice complained, and the man who'd sat over him on the long funeral ride leaned close, yanking off the shades he'd worn and staring down at Ray intently. Ray watched back, seeing only hard-edged anger in the man's eyes.

Pulling away and tucking an arm of the glasses into the neck of his shirt, the man muttered, "His jawin' don't bother me none."

Ray needed to purge this bubble of guilt inside him before they ended him. It felt vital that they understand at least a little of what he'd carried inside him all this time.

"She was my sanity. I needed her so I could stay sane. I tried with so many others, but they never did it for me like she did. She was like a box I could stuff that sick shit in, and she'd lock it up tight. Keep it locked up for a long time."

She gave me rest. Real rest, the kind that lasted.

Sticks and sand shoved under the bottom edges of his vest and shirt as the men hauled him along the ground.

"Gotta take the vest off. It's got that shit bull riders wear."

"She went away." Ray tipped his head, uncaring of the rocks and stones his skull and body hit as he stared up into the man's face. "So I tried to find that with so many others. I couldn't find what I needed. That peace. I looked, man. *You gotta know I looked.* Never found another box like her. She's something special. Fixed the monster in me, the monster my old man made me into."

He twisted to see they were nearing a gully. A rabbit broke cover, and with long jumps, streaked away out of sight.

Run, bunny. Run away. I can't, so you gotta run for me.

"You got no idea how it feels to live with this inside me. It's always hated me, couldn't get away from me any more than I could escape it." The dragging stopped and he sucked in a deep breath. "When the hell you live in is inside you, what do you do?"

A hand wrenched at his vest and he heard snaps and stitching give way. Struck by a massive jolt of fear, he reflexively blurted something that often woke him up at night. The realization his plague had bled out onto so many more people than he'd killed.

"The families. They'll never know." Arching his neck, he glared up. "They gotta know."

"On three." That was the driver's voice again, and Ray watched as the man standing in front of him reached to the small of his back and brought out a gun. "One."

"Gotta know what, asshole?" Leveling the weapon, the tall man's expression was impassive behind his graying beard. His vest label said Horse.

A horse, of course.

The errant thought didn't make sense and Ray tried to focus, terror making his body shake. He was afraid for the first time in a while. Not of dying, but of not expressing this thought that held the utmost importance.

"Two."

Ray looked into the bleak darkness of the barrel, remembering the long hallway that led to his childhood window, and took a breath.

"Where they're buried."

Three.

~

Afterword

THANK YOU FOR READING
Ray Nelms: A Study in Insanity!

ABOUT THE AUTHOR

Raised in the south, *Wall Street Journal* & *USA TODAY* bestselling author MariaLisa learned about the magic of books at an early age. Every summer, she would spend hours in the local library, devouring books of every genre. Self-described as a book-a-holic, she says "I've always loved to read, but then I discovered writing, and found I adored that, too. For reading...if nothing else is available, I've been known to read the back of the cereal box."

More info and extras about her books can be found on **mldemora.com**.

Want sneak peeks into what she's working on, or to chat with other readers about her books? Join the Facebook group! **bit.ly/deMora-FB-group**

deMora's got a spam-free newsletter list she'd love to have you join, too: **bit.ly/mldemora-newsletter**

~~~~~
~~~~~

ADDITIONAL SERIES AND BOOKS

Please note that books in a series frequently feature characters from additional books within that series. If series books are read out of order, readers will twig to spoilers for the other books, so going back to read the skipped titles won't have the same angsty reveals.

Freed Riders MC

Born from characters who simply wouldn't allow their stories to die, this spin-off series includes men and women who will be familiar to the RWMC and NTNT fans.

> *Gotta Dig Deep*, #1
> *Always My Fate*, #2 (coming soon)
> *Somewhere in Texas,* #3 (coming soon)

Rebel Wayfarers crossover stories

Enjoy these stories that tie the different worlds of my ever-growing MC universe together, bringing Rebel Wayfarers MC and clubs like those in Freed Riders, Neither This Nor That, and other series into glorious alignment.

Going Down Easy
No Man's Land
In Search of Solace
Ray Nelms: A Study in Insanity

Rebel Wayfarers MC series

A motorcycle club can be a frightening place, filled with hardened men and bad attitudes. Rebel Wayfarers is a club with their own measure of hard and dangerous, led by their national president, Davis Mason. This book series follows members as they move through their lives, filled with anguish and heartache, laughter and love. In the club, each of them find a home and family they thought long lost to them.

Mica, #1
A Sweet & Merry Christmas, #1.5
Slate, #2
Bear, #3
Jase, #4
Gunny, #5
Mason, #6
Hoss, #7
Harddrive Holidays, #7.5
Duck, #8
Biker Chick Campout, #8.5
Watcher, #9
A Kiss to Keep You, #9.25
Gun Totin' Annie, #9.5
Secret Santa, #9.75
Bones, #10
Gunny's Pups, #10.25
Not Even A Mouse, #10.75

Fury, #11
Christmas Doings, #11.25
Gypsy's Lady includes *Never Settle* (#10.5),
#11.5
Cassie, #12
Road Runner's Ride, #12.5

Occupy Yourself band series

Stardom doesn't happen overnight. Hell, it doesn't even happen after a decade in the business, as the members of Occupy Yourself have found out. But, with the right talent and the right representation, they might still have a chance to make it big. As long as they can keep their lead singer sober, keep their drummer focused on the music, keep their guitarist out of trouble … well, you get the idea. Come and join us, stand side stage for a close-up view of the backstage happenings in a rock-and-roll band. It's guaranteed to be a show you won't ever forget.

Born Into Trouble, #1
Grace In Motion, #2 (TBD)
What They Say, #3 (TBD)

Neither This, Nor That MC series

Legends are born from moments like these. Folktales spun around a single point in time so perfect, you can almost hear the click resonating through the universe as things align. Meet Twisted, Po'Boy, Retro, and Ragman, good old boys from southern states who have many things in common. First, is a bone-deep love of the biker lifestyle. Second, would be their love of the brotherhood, and knowing that you trust the man at your back. Finally, these men have the love of a good woman. None of these come without a price, and it is our pleasure to journey along with them as they discover the blessings that can be won, and lost a ong the way.

Rogue Maniacs MC

With a first book set within the collaborative worlds of the Mayhem Makers, these stories will introduce brand new characters and tales.

Downward Dawg, #1
Raggedy Dan, #2 (coming soon)
Tinder Heart, #3 (coming soon)

Mayhan Bucklers MC series

The Mayhan Bucklers MC has been part of the rolling hills of Northeast Texas for decades. Now, new life is being breathed into this reborn club, a legacy resurrected by grandsons of the founder. The MBMC is set to surpass its original glory, fortified with an honorable purpose: Helping wounded warriors reintegrate back into society, gifting those who've given so much with a safe place to land.

Learning how to navigate life while war still echoes inside you isn't easy, but with solid brothers at your back, anything is possible.

Most Rikki-Tik, #1
Mad Minute, #2
Pucker Factor, #3
Boocoo Dinky Dau, #4

Borderline Freaks MC series

When you can't count on anyone else to save you, there's only one real choice. Borderline Freaks MC is a series of books about the men of the club and their brotherhood — and of course the love they have for their women. Take a trip along with Monk, Blade, Wolf, and Neptune, and feel for yourself the connection these men have for each other.

Service and Sacrifice, #1
More Than Enough, #2
Lack of In-between, #3
See You in Valhalla, #4

Alace Sweets series

Dark romantic thrillers, these books are not light reads. Filled with edge-of-your-seat suspense, these intense stories command the reader's attention as they drive towards their explosive endings. Alace Sweets is a vigilante serial killer, with everything that implies and is sure to trip all your triggers. Be ready.

Alace Sweets, #1
Seeking Worthy Pursuits, #2
Embarrassment of Monsters, #3
All the Broken Rules, #4 (TBD)

With My Whole Heart series

Sweet as pie and twice as delicious, these romantic love stories are a guaranteed happily-ever-after read.

With My Whole Heart, #1
Bet On Us, #2

If You Could Change One Thing: Tangled Fates Stories

When threads in the tapestry of life are cut short, inexorably changing the future for those you love, would you be willing to tempt fate to set things right?

There Are Limits, #1
Rules Are Rules, #2
The Gray Zone, #3

Additional Books:

Hard Focus
Dirty Bitches MC: Season 3

~~~~~
~~~~~

deMora's Rebel Wayfarers MC and the Neither This Nor That MC series do cross over, along with the Occupy Yourself band books, so readers have a couple of choices. The series can be read independently beginning with RWMC, OYBS, and then NTNT without too many spoilers. There's also a crossover between deMora's RWMC world and Lila Rose's Hawks MC world. Or they can be read intertwined—in chronological order.

Here's the recommended reading order if you want to follow according to timing:

Mica, RWMC #1
A Sweet & Merry Christmas, RWMC #1.5
Slate, RWMC #2
Bear, RWMC #3
Born Into Trouble, OYBS #1
Jase, RWMC #4
Gunny, RWMC #5
Mason, RWMC #6
Hoss, RWMC #7
This Is the Route of Twisted Pain, NTNT #1
Harddrive Holidays, RWMC #7.5
Duck, RWMC #8
Biker Chick Campout, RWMC #8.5
Watcher, RWMC #9
Treading the Traitor's Path: Out Bad, NTNT #2

Living Without, Lila Rose's Hawks MC: Caroline Springs #4
Shelter My Heart, NTNT #3
A Kiss to Keep You, RWMC #9.25
Gun Totin' Annie, RWMC #9.5
Secret Santa, RWMC #9.75
Trapped by Fate on Reckless Roads, NTNT #4
Bones, RWMC #10
Gunny's Pups, RWMC #10.25
Not Even A Mouse, RWMC #10.75
Road Runner's Ride, RWMC #12.5
Never Settle, RWMC #10.5
Fury, RWMC #11
Christmas Doings, RWMC #11.25
Gypsy's Lady, RWMC #11.5
Tarnished Lies and Dead Ends, NTNT #5
Going Down Easy
No Man's Land
In Search of Solace
Tangled Threats on the Nomad Highway, NTNT #6
Cassie, RWMC #12

More information available at
mldemora.com.

www.ingramcontent.com/pod-product-compliance
Lightning Source LLC
Chambersburg PA
CBHW070519200726
48293CB00007B/2603